A
GIRAFFE
AND A HALF

by Shel Silverstein

HarperCollins*Publishers*

ISBN 0-590-47164-3

21   05 06 07

Printed in Mexico   49

First Scholastic printing, January 1993

If you had a giraffe...

and he stretched

another half...

you would have

a giraffe and a half.

If he put on a hat
and inside lived a rat...

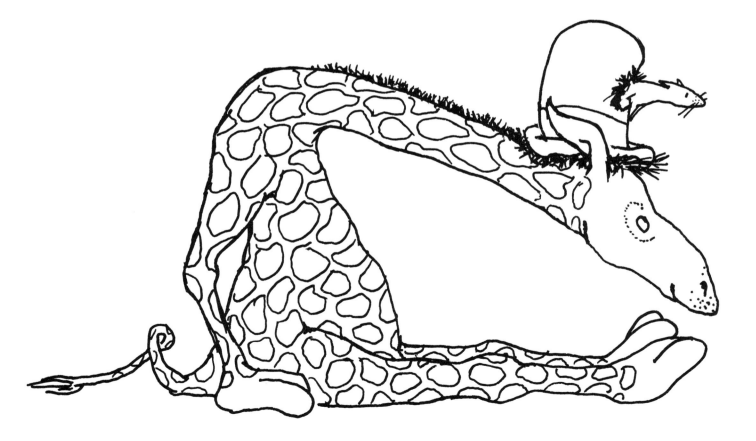

you would have a giraffe and a half
with a rat in his hat.

If you dressed him in a suit
and he looked very cute...

you would have a giraffe and a half
with a rat in his hat
looking cute in a suit.

If you glued a rose
to the tip of his nose...

you would have a giraffe and a half
with a rat in his hat
looking cute in a suit
with a rose on his nose.

If a bumbley old bee
stung him right on the knee...

you would have a giraffe and a half
with a rat in his hat
looking cute in a suit
with a rose on his nose
and a bee on his knee.

If he put on a shoe
and then stepped in some glue...

you would have a giraffe and a half
with a rat in his hat
looking cute in a suit
with a rose on his nose
and a bee on his knee
and some glue on his shoe.

If you gave him a flute
and he played tooty-toot...

you would have a giraffe and a half
with a rat in his hat
looking cute in a suit
with a rose on his nose
and a bee on his knee
and some glue on his shoe
playing toot on a flute.

If he used a chair
to comb his hair...

you would have a giraffe and a half
with a rat in his hat
looking cute in a suit
with a rose on his nose
and a bee on his knee
and some glue on his shoe
playing toot on a flute
with a chair in his hair.

If he tripped on a snake
who was eating some cake...

you would have a giraffe and a half
with a rat in his hat
looking cute in a suit
with a rose on his nose
and a bee on his knee
and some glue on his shoe
playing toot on a flute
with a chair in his hair
and a snake eating cake.

If he found an old trunk
and inside was a skunk...

you would have a giraffe and a half
with a rat in his hat
looking cute in a suit
with a rose on his nose
and a bee on his knee
and some glue on his shoe
playing toot on a flute
with a chair in his hair
and a snake eating cake
and a skunk in a trunk.

If he met a fat dragon
who sat in a wagon...

you would have a giraffe and a half
with a rat in his hat
looking cute in a suit
with a rose on his nose
and a bee on his knee
and some glue on his shoe
playing toot on a flute
with a chair in his hair
and a snake eating cake
and a skunk in a trunk
and a dragon in a wagon.

If he jumped on a bike
and rode over a spike...

you would have a giraffe and a half
with a rat in his hat
looking cute in a suit
with a rose on his nose
and a bee on his knee
and some glue on his shoe
playing toot on a flute
with a chair in his hair
and a snake eating cake
and a skunk in a trunk
and a dragon in a wagon
and a spike in his bike.

If a blubbery whale
got ahold of his tail . . .

you would have a giraffe and a half
with a rat in his hat
looking cute in a suit
with a rose on his nose
and a bee on his knee
and some glue on his shoe
playing toot on a flute
with a chair in his hair
and a snake eating cake
and a skunk in a trunk
and a dragon in a wagon
and a spike in his bike
and a whale on his tail.

If he fell in a hole
that was dug by a mole...

you would have a giraffe and a half
with a rat in his hat
looking cute in a suit
with a rose on his nose
and a bee on his knee
and some glue on his shoe
playing toot on a flute
with a chair in his hair
and a snake eating cake
and a skunk in a trunk
and a dragon in a wagon
and a spike in his bike
and a whale on his tail
in a hole with a mole.

But . . . if you brought him a pole
to climb out of the hole . . .

and the whale left his tail
and went off for the mail...

and he gave the spiked bike
to a scout on a hike...

and he left the fat dragon
'cause his wagon was saggin'...

and he gave his chair
to a tired old bear...

and he traded the flute
to a bird for some fruit . . .

and he told that old snake
to go jump in the lake...

and a man who bought junk
bought the trunk with the skunk...

and he gave the rose
to a girl he chose...

while the bee on his knee
flew away with a flea...

and he put the shoe
with the glue
on *you* . . .

and that silly old rat
ran away with his hat...

and he put his suit
in the laundry chute...

and he shrank another half...

you would have a giraffe!